Why Elephant has a Trunk

Series created by
Claudia Lloyd

This Booktime book belongs to

. . . .

PUFFIN

Text based on the script written by Edward Gakuya and Claudia Lloyd.

Illustrations from the TV animation produced by Tiger Aspect Productions Limited and Homeboyz Entertainment Kenya.

Artwork supplied by Celestine Wamiru.

PUFFIN BOOKS:
Published by the Penguin Group: London, New York,
Australia, Canada, India, Ireland, New Zealand and South
Africa. Penguin Books Ltd, Registered Offices: 80 Strand, London
WC2R 0RL, England. Published in Puffin Books 2010.
This edition published on behalf of Pearson
in association with Booktrust for Booktime 2011

Printed and bound in China by
Absolutely Publishing and Media Ltd

This title is printed on FSC-certified paper

British Library Cataloguing in Publication Data
A CIP catalogue record for this book is available
from the British Library

001 – 10 9 8 7 6 5 4 3 2 1

ISBN: 978–0–141–33986–3

You see there was a time
when Elephant had no nose.
He was **big.**
He was **clumsy.**
AND he was very, very **smelly.**

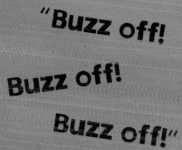

"Buzz off!
Buzz off!
Buzz off!"

And wherever Elephant went,
the **flies** went too!

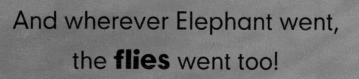

So Elephant asked the Monkeys for help.

"**Jambo**, **Monkeys!** Do you know how to make these **flies** go away?"

"Why don't you try
having a good old **wa**–"

". . . **walk** in the bush!"

"**That** should
get rid of the **flies.**"

"Thank you, **Monkeys**, I will."
And Elephant walked off into the bush.

"Monkeys, you should have told Elephant the truth. Some beast really ought to tell him that he smells . . . **very pongy!**" said Lion.

"Elephant doesn't **know** how much he smells because he's got **no nose**," said Tortoise.

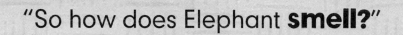

"So how does Elephant **smell?**"

"**Terrible!**"

"Hee heee heeee!"

Lion looked at Tortoise. "Tortoise, you **are** his **oldest** friend . . ."

"Very well, I'll tell Elephant **straight away . . .**" And Tortoise went to look for Elephant.

Deep in the bush
Elephant came across
Chameleon.

"**Jambo**, Chameleon! These flies
are driving me **crazy!**"

"I'm **sorry?**"
said Elephant.

"Well, flies like **stinky**
things, my friend,"
said Chameleon.

...**smelly!**"

"**Ooooh!**" said Elephant sadly.

"Well, you **do** have a slight problem in the **whiffy** department. You're a bit, you know...

"But don't go getting all upset," said Chameleon. "It's nothing a good **scrub** won't fix."

"But I **can't** scrub!" said Elephant.

"I can't reach behind my **ears.**

I can't reach my **back.**

"Sorry, I can't help, Elephant ..."

"Well, thank you for being
so **honest**, Chameleon,"
said Elephant.

I can't even reach my **belly!**"

And off he went to look for
his old friend **Tortoise** ...

"Oops . . . **there** you are, Tortoise!"

"**Jambo**, **Elephant.**
Why do you look so sad?"

"Tortoise, we've known each
other a very long time . . .
Why didn't you ever tell me
that I . . . **smell?**"

"Well, have you ever thought of
taking a **bath?**" asked Tortoise.

"No. That's **brilliant!**"
said Elephant. "Why didn't
I think of that?"

So Elephant and Tortoise went back to the waterhole.

"**Jambo**, **Hippo**," said Elephant.
"Chameleon says I **smell**, and Tortoise
says maybe I should have a **bath.**
So could I wash in your
waterhole, please?"

"**Of course**, Elephant!" said Hippo.
"Come on in. The water's **LOVELY!**"

But just as Elephant was about to get in the water . . .

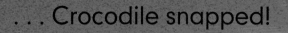

. . . Crocodile snapped!

"SNAP!"

"Don't even **THINK** of coming in my waterhole!"

"Ohhh, but I don't **want** to **smell!**" said Elephant.

"Don't worry," said Hippo. "Crocodile will swim off downriver in the morning. You can have a bath **tomorrow!**"

"Try to get some **sleep**," said Tortoise.

"Watch out for **Crocodile** though," warned Tickbird. "He's so **snappy** at the moment. **Snappy, snappy, SNAPPY!**"

Night fell and Owl flew down
to comfort Elephant.

"Sniff" "Sniff"

"**Oh, Owl**," said Elephant, "the Monkeys **laugh** at me. Chameleon says I **smell.** Tortoise thinks I should have a **bath**, but Crocodile **won't let me!** And I can't even blow my **nose!**"

"I know it seems bad, Elephant," said Owl, "but sometimes **good things come from bad.** Trust me."

So Elephant fell asleep.

Then suddenly there was an enormous . . .

The animals heard Elephant shouting and rushed to help him.

"It's **Elephant!**"

"**Haraka! Haraka!** Quickly! Quickly!"

"Crocodile, **stop it!** Stop it **right now!**" shouted Hippo.

"**Mamba!**" roared Lion. "**CROCODILE!**"

"Stop talking,
start pulling!"
called Tickbird.

So all the animals **pulled...**

...and they **pulled**...

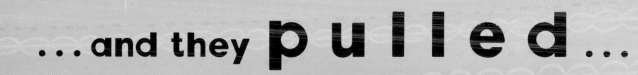

...and they p u l l e d...

And Elephant's nose got

longer

and **longer**

and **longer** until . . .

KER-DOING!

All the animals landed in
a big Tinga Tinga heap!

"**Look at my nose!**" said Elephant.
"It's all **long** and **wiggly!**

Hmmmm . . . I wonder . . . "

Elephant tried **swatting away** the **flies** with his new long nose.

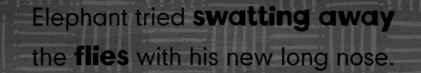

"Buzz off!"

"Buzz off!"

And the flies **buzzed off!**

Then Elephant took a lovely **big shower** with his new long nose.

It was a **very useful wiggly nose indeed!**

"Look! I'm clean!
No more smell!"
shouted Elephant happily.

"I bet you can **blow** your new nose too!" said Owl.

"TeRRRRUmpett!"

"I can! **I can blow my new nose!**" trumpeted Elephant.

"And what are you going to **call** your new nose, Elephant?" said Owl . . .

"**A trunk!** I'm going to call it a . . .

. . .**TRUNK!**"

So you see, Owl was **right** . . .
sometimes **good things do come from bad.**

And that's **why Elephant has a trunk.**